DWENNON'S DESPAIR

A GHOST WALKER SHORT STORY

ALEXANDRIA BLAELOCK

BlueMere Books
MELBOURNE, AUSTRALIA

For permission requests, please contact
enquiries@bluemerebooks.com.

Ordering Information:
Discounts are available on quantity purchases. For details, contact orders@bluemerebooks.com.

Dwennon's Despair/Alexandria Blaelock
paperback ISBN: 978-1-922744-31-9
digital ISBN: 978-1-922744-32-6

BlueMere Books
www.bluemerebooks.com

DWENNON'S DESPAIR

Dwennon adjusted his hat as he looked in the mirror.

Was it maybe a little too bright? Or perhaps a shade too pink?

He couldn't tell. Though he could see the pink reflected well on his light skin and dark hair

Plus, it brought attention to his hard, square, manly jaw and muscular body.

He turned this way and that, admiring his blurry reflection in the flickering candlelight, wishing for a mirror with a clearer reflection.

The pink hat looked good on him, but did that mean he should wear it?

He dipped a piece of stale bread into his cup of watered wine and looked at the hat again as he chewed.

Was the colour sufficiently stunning? Did he need to add some jewels or feathers to spruce it up a bit?

Or maybe tone it down - he was wearing a bright orange tunic after all.

It wouldn't do his career any good to outshine Prince Indulf in his own Court. The trick was to stay just enough ahead of the rest of them.

He turned, lip curling, to look at the pile of clothing he'd thrown on the flagstone floor.

It really didn't help that someone or something had sneaked into his room, gone into his clothing press and torn up his clothing.

It could, of course, be repaired.

But that would mean starting a new fashion for shorter, slimmer tunics and he wasn't entirely sure the Court was ready for that.

He leapt over the pile of tunics he'd discarded on the floor and threw himself onto the bed.

It wasn't fair.

He'd been sent to Court, to find a compliant rich Lady to marry. Her money would shore up the family fortunes, and he would hopefully live in peace and quiet in a small corner of the family seat for the rest of his life.

Becoming the talk of the Court for his flamboyant clothing style had not been part of that plan.

Admittedly, as the third son of a minor noble, he had very little to commend himself to the rich Ladies of the Court.

And it was possible that being talked about was better than not being talked about, but the pressure of always being distinctive was tremendous.

Always trying to not stray over that thick grey line that would see him disgraced and banished from Court.

And perhaps cost the family its lands.

That would go down like a giant lead fishing weight.

For that matter, Dwennon's clothing problems had been non-existent before he'd arrived at Court.

He'd don his never-changing plain and practical clothing, and spend the long days alone, hunting and fishing to keep the family well stocked with meat and fish.

If he'd had his way, he wouldn't be at Court at all, he'd be back home, coursing for deer with the hounds.

Not cooped up inside, worrying about what was messing with his clothes overnight.

He called it the *Vestitus Demon* because it snuck into his clothes press and changed his clothes overnight. Sometimes just the colour. Or from velvet to silk and back again. Or cut them shorter.

Or even more bizarrely, longer.

It had only been a few weeks, but already it felt like an eternity, the sooner he found a wife and got out of there, the better.

Too late to run away now though.

Grudgingly, he acknowledged that the demon generally made sure he had an attractive and appropriate outfit no matter how outlandish.

And didn't mess with his hunting equipment or armoury.

Just the clothes.

And hats, shoes, and now and again his limited collection of jewellery.

But only to create outfits.

After a time, the glamour or whatever it was wore off and his clothes reverted to their original appearance.

Until the next time.

He leaned off the bed and picked a blue silk tunic up from the floor for a closer look.

What he'd initially taken for gaping holes had been neatly hemmed. He happened to notice that while it was unexpected, the blue was a good match for the untorn orange he was wearing.

Sighing he stood up, took the hat off and pulled the blue tunic on over the orange. When he put the hat back on, he could tell it was too much, and looked in the press to see if there was anything else that might work.

And of course, there was.

A kind of floppy, flat-topped black hat. With a spray of blue and orange ribbons.

Naturally.

Dwennon sighed.

Definitely no escaping the festivities tonight then.

Which actually was never going to happen regardless of what the clothing demon threw at him.

Maybe demon wasn't the right word, but he was pretty sure angels didn't go around remaking people's wardrobes overnight.

One last doubtful look in the mirror and he left the room.

Almost immediately, he rocked back on his heels to avoid Mrs Godwaine the Housekeeper as she swept passed the room chased by some kind of filthy servant girl.

Good luck to the girl, Mrs Godwaine was a fearsome woman, and he wasn't the only one that turned and walked quickly away whenever he saw her coming.

The girl met his eyes for a moment, then turned away, as if she knew what he was thinking and didn't like it.

He felt judged and found wanting.

Which irritated him given he was noble, and she was nothing.

After a moment to let his heartbeat slow down, he headed down to the main hall to hang around with the other courtiers.

As he was confined to the outer rooms, he could relax a little, and hang around with the other younger sons.

Not getting up to mischief *per se*, but getting away with the kind of things you couldn't do in the inner rooms.

Which was actually where he needed to be to win a rich Lady.

Only the married women were in the outer court, presumably to protect the young and innocent ones from men like him.

Arriving at the entrance to the outer hall, he saw his friends were already there. Jerald, Beval and Silas were also ran sons like him.

It wasn't unheard of for a third son to inherit the title, but unusual.

So unusual that none of them had any practical or useful skills.

Society being what it was, the only careers open to them were soldier, farmer or court adviser.

Though the careers were more of obligations to the King than actual income opportunities.

Beval had been at Court for several years, and his father was threatening him with the priesthood if he didn't bring home a suitable bride this season.

Dwennon absolutely did not want to enter the priesthood, but Jerald preferred that to the army.

Dwennon didn't want to enter the army either, he just wanted to be a farmer.

He just needed to sort out the dratted wife thing so he could go home.

He straightened his shoulders and took a deep breath.

Then let it out as he sauntered through the door.

His friends saw him almost immediately, and clustered around him peppering him with questions about his outfit.

"Well *woodness*," said Silas, "that's another fine outfit, how did you come up with that?"

"I keep telling you *wind-sucker* the *Vestitus Demon* puts them in my clothes press."

"*Fopdoodle!*" said Jerald, "there's no such thing as a *Vestitus Demon*. And in any case, a demon would ruin your clothes."

"Have you seen what I'm wearing? This is hundreds of hundreds of leagues from the clothes I brought with me."

Beval laughed, "who's the *fopdoodle* now?

"Oh! That reminds me, did you hear the Prince brought a Ghost Walker to court?"

They all turned to Beval, eyes wide.

"A Ghost Walker?" asked Jerald, "I didn't think there were any left."

"You wouldn't think so given the Church has been hunting and burning them for decades," answered Silas.

"True," said Beval, "but I expect the villagers would have got in first."

"Are they demons or people do you think?" Dwennon wondered.

"I heard they can disappear from one place and reappear in another, so I expect that makes them demons," said Jerald.

"I think they're just dirty lying peasants who can hide really well when other peasants try to catch and kill them," answered Beval.

They all laughed.

But Dwennon was fascinated.

What would it be like to be surrounded by dead people all the time?

Technically he was already surrounded by dead people, but he couldn't see them, so he didn't generally think about them.

He wondered idly if anyone had followed him from home.

Oddly enough, not being alone was a comforting thought.

What if it was a dead relative messing with his clothes? Who could it be?

And then it hit him, that perhaps a Ghost Walker could help him with his demon.

He either had to find his own or get deeper into Court to meet the Prince's. And finding his own seemed easier.

"How do you think the Prince found it?" he asked.

"Well, I don't think you can take the dogs out and hunt them like deer," Silas answered, slapping him on the back.

Beval frowned, "That's not how politics works.

"He'd've quietly put the word out, and someone somewhere would've said something, and someone else said something more and eventually he'd get the answer back.

"Then he'd send someone else out to get the Walker before it could move on."

They were silent for a moment.

"Do you think he's arrested it and is torturing it in a dungeon somewhere?" Dwennon asked.

Jerald laughed, "That's the wrong question my friend, the bigger question is why he defied the Church to find one and bring it to Court. What could be so important that he'd risk the Crown?"

"No," said Dwennon, "he's a Goist. The Church is only here in an ambassadorial function."

His friends looked at him with raised eyebrows.

He shrugged one shoulder, "We're Goists too."

Beval grunted, "That's an interesting twist. Would the Prince hand it over to the Church when he's got what he wanted, or let it go?"

"Why would he do either of those things?" Silas asked. "If he felt the need to get one in the first place, why wouldn't he keep it?

"Maybe install it in some kind of official capacity, or give it some kind of high domestic position like Mrs Godwaine?"

They shuddered in unison at the thought of the Royal Housekeeper.

"Do you think he can protect it? Keep it safe from the Church?" asked Dwennon.

Silas scratched his chin, "Well, we know he's got one, but not whether it's male or female, young or old, noble or common.

"I guess the Church would have spies who could find out. But would they defy the ruling family and risk expulsion from the country?"

Beval frowned, "or would they use this as leverage to incite a rebellion and overthrow the Royal family?"

Dwennon sucked in his breath and held his stomach in both hands, "Could they? I thought this was a country where religions of all kinds were tolerated."

Jerald patted his shoulder, "you're so soft. All religions are run by ambitious men, they all want power, and they all want to rule the world."

"Indeed" said Silas, "even if the Prince expels the Church, that won't be the end of it. There will still be fanatics in the country who will take matters into their own hands."

"Politics eh?" said Dwennon. "Thank goodness I'll not need to worry about it."

《《 • 》》

Dwennon realised he'd lived a relatively sheltered life.

These machinations filled him with dread. That one or two people could ruin it for everyone was monstrous.

He wondered if he should warn the Prince.

Not that he had any idea how to get close to the Prince.

In any case, the Prince must have some idea of the danger, and a plan to deal with it - he was The Prince after all.

He needed some spiritual solace and decided on a visit to the temple.

Happily, the *Vestitus Demon* provided some appropriately sombre dark blue and black clothing to wear.

Leaving his shoes and hat at the door, Dwennon entered the temple and knelt, bare head bowed, in front of the giant gilded statue of the Praeceptor

He closed his eyes and let the peace of countless generations of meditators soak into his body while he waited for the Praeceptor's wisdom to reach him.

After a time, he became aware of a presence beside him. It didn't talk or move, and he wasn't sure whether it was also meditating or waiting for him.

He opened one eye and saw a short-haired young woman in the black robes of a Goist nun. She looked vaguely familiar though he didn't know where from.

She was very still and seemed deeply peaceful.

She cocked her head and smiled conspiratorially at him.

He was smitten.

He couldn't help himself, he smiled back.

She rose and left the temple, and as if she'd pulled a string, he followed her.

They sat, side by side, on a bench in the porch, looking out over the contemplation garden.

She didn't say anything, just waited in a silent invitation for him to tell her his concerns.

He struggled to come up with a way to express them.

"I heard some things that have me worried."

She nodded but didn't reply.

"I heard that the Prince may have done something that could open him and the Kingdom to a Church led rebellion."

She nodded again, seemingly untroubled by his concern.

"I heard he'd brought a Ghost Walker to Court."

She looked at him sharply.

"I don't know who or what it is, but in Church countries, they burn them as heretics."

She frowned.

"I'm worried that if the Church finds out, they'll do something to overthrow the throne and burn them both."

Her face went hard. She stood and walked away without saying a word.

He reached for her as she left, but missed.

And decided the wisest course of action was to let her go.

He'd wanted to get word to the Prince, and a Goist nun was probably an easier and more effective way than trying to get into the Prince's Inner Circle.

But she was so pretty.

Well, not pretty really.

Striking?

Handsome?

She certainly had a presence that hinted at hidden practical depths.

Unlike the Court Ladies of his acquaintance, she felt like she'd roll her sleeves up and get on with whatever it was that needed doing.

In fact, she seemed the best of both worlds. At home at Court as well as getting down and dirty on the farm.

He wondered whether she'd committed to the temple for life, or just for a time.

He wondered whether she'd consider giving it up for a life with him.

Then he wondered if he could give up everything he knew for a life with her.

《《 • 》》

The days and weeks passed, and Dwennon had not seen the nun. He'd been to temple almost every day, looking for her instead of paying attention to his prayers.

He was thinking about her, not the hunt, when his horse bolted, spooked by something in the bushes.

He was thrown from the saddle, and with a painful and loud crack, broke his leg.

Fortunately, the horse wasn't injured, but it'd be months before he'd ride again.

Dwennon was happy his father hadn't called him back home, though he knew the journey would probably be a nightmare that would likely end in his death on the way.

In the meantime, he decided to visit the library to see what he could find out about the Ghost Walkers.

He'd limped on his incredibly uncomfortable crutches, and was about ready to pass out from the pain when he opened the door and collapsed onto a chair just inside the entrance.

He felt dizzy for a moment and was about to slip off the chair when he was caught in the strong arms of the nun.

"You're here!" he said.

She smiled slightly and helped him back onto the chair.

He blanked out for a bit, then she was there, one arm around his shoulder supporting his weight and the other holding a cup of watered wine to his lips.

He took a sip.

"Are you all right now?" she asked.

He nodded and took another sip, before sighing and closing his eyes.

"You had me worried for a moment there."

He opened his eyes to see her face just inches away from his. "I've been looking for you."

"I know."

"How?"

She pointed her chin to the left, "they told me."

He looked where she'd pointed and saw blurry people shaped blobs.

He rubbed his eyes and looked again, but they weren't any clearer.

"Are they ghosts?"

She nodded once.

"Are you the Ghost Walker then?"

She nodded again.

"Then can you tell me why my clothes keep changing?"

She laughed and left him to sit up on his own. "Of all possible things, that's what you want to know?"

He nodded.

She folded her hands in her lap, looked towards the ghosts and went still.

Then she snorted and blushed.

"It's your grandmother. Did you know she was part Elvish?"

He crinkled his nose and leaned away from her, trying to decide if she was telling the truth or playing a trick on him.

"Are you really a nun?"

"Yes, why?"

"Just trying to work out if you're telling the truth."

"Why would I lie about your grandmother?"

"Who knows these days."

"Yes, I suppose. Though you don't need to worry about that. The Prince has it in hand."

"That's good news.

"Now about my elvish grandmother. What has she got to do with my clothes?"

"Ah. Yes. She likes your *Vestitus* nickname by the way."

Dwennon smiled, "I thought it was a good one.

"Oh— Do you mean she's the one changing them? Why would she do that?"

"Well, she's trying to attract my attention."

"Your attention? Why would she do that?"

"Oh, you're such a *fopdoodle!* Why does anyone's grandmother normally get herself involved in their life?"

"Oh," Dwennon blushed, "you mean..."

"Yes exactly. She's matchmaking."

"She wants you and me to..."

"Exactly."

Dwennon looked at his feet, "Well. I...

"I...

"I would be happy to follow her suggestion in this matter."

The nun laughed again, "I don't know her, why should I follow her suggestion?"

"Oh.

"Did you have any plans of your own?"

"No, but that's beside the point. What do you have to offer that I should give up my place and follow you to the country?"

She flapped her hand in the direction of the ghosts as if shushing them.

"You don't have to give up your place. I'll give up mine and stay here with you."

"I've taken vows of poverty and chastity."

"I'll wait until you're ready to leave the ministry."

"You don't know anything about me."

"No, but I knew my grandmother.

"She's clever, observant, and gave good advice. Even if she's dead, I still trust her.

"If she thinks you're the right one for me, I'd rather rely on her judgement than take a chance on my own."

She tilted her head to one side and looked at him for a long time.

"She seems to have garnered a deal of respect from the resident ghosts since she's been here.

"I'm not agreeing Dwennon, I'm just giving you the chance to convince me."

He smiled. "Then, perhaps as a gesture of good faith, you could tell me your name."

She laughed, "my name is Alma."

"Well Alma," he took a hand from her lap and held it in both of his, "I'm very pleased to meet you."

THE END

ABOUT THE AUTHOR

Alexandria Blaelock writes stories, some of them for *Ellery Queen's Mystery Magazine* and *Pulphouse Fiction Magazine*. She's also written four self-help books applying business techniques to personal matters like getting dressed, cleaning house, and feeding your friends.

As a recovering Project Manager, she's probably too fond of sticking to plan. She lives in a forest because she enjoys birdsong, the scent of gum leaves and the sun on her face. When not telecommuting to parallel universes from her Melbourne based imagination, she watches K-dramas, talks to animals, and drinks Campari. At the same time.

Discover more at www.alexandriablaelock.com.

BOOKS BY
ALEXANDRIA BLAELOCK

SHORT STORY COLLECTIONS

The Histories of Hayward Hall
Lovelorn, Lovestruck and Love at First Sight
Common or Garden Variety Heroes
Case Files of the Wilkinson Detective Agency
Unavoidable Fates
Christmas Travesties
Five Faces of Felicia Clarke

OTHER FICTION

That Love Nonsense

MS BLAELOCK'S BOOKS

Stress Free Dinner Parties
Signature Wardrobe Planning
Holistic Personal Finance
Minimally Viable Housekeeping
Planning a Life Worth Living

SELECTED SHORT STORIES

Alma's Grace
Balancing the Book
Carmelita Basingstoke
Fate in Your Hands
Kiss of Death
Lady of the Looking Glass
Life in the Security Directorate
Long Weekend in the Snow
Love in the Past Tense
Love in the Security Directorate
Morning Star, Evening Star, Superstar
Needy Bitch
Payton's Run
Phoenix Child
Secret Singer
Shining Star
Ship in a Bottle
Simone Says Hands in the Air
Special Relativity in Space
The Bygone Boyfriend
The Day the Schedule Broke
The Ghost Detectors
The Guardian's Vigil
The Mince Pie Mystery
The Mystery of the Master Suite
The Pseudonym's Bride
The Shadow Thieves
The Time-Space Paradox
Toy Soldiers